MOTHER EARTH'S DAY
BY ETHAN AYODEJI STEPHEN

EDITED BY
TINUOLA
STEPHEN-FAGBEMIGUN

MOTHER EARTH'S DAY

Published by: Tinuola Stephen-Fagbemigun,
Edmonton, Canada

Author: Ethan Ayodeji Stephen
Editor: Tinuola Stephen-Fagbemigun.
Illustrator: Martin Avwenagha

ISBN
 Paperback 11 x 8.5   978-1-77354-639-1
 Paperback 8.5 x 8.5   978-1-77354-618-6
  Hardcover   978-1-77354-637-7

Publication assistance by

PAGEMASTER
PUBLISHING
PageMaster.ca

Ethan Ayodeji Stephen

A long time ago the earth was beautifully green with plants and water.

It is almost Mother Earth Day.

Now when the heavens looked down they saw waste creating stress on Mother Earth.

Mother Earth's friends and siblings sat together to plan on how to help, and to celebrate Mother Earth.

Stary said, "Mother Earth would be happy if we can do all we can to keep her clean, and then we can have a party to celebrate.

Moony asked, "What can we do to make mother Earth happy before the party?"

One of them said, "we can recycle."

Another one said, "we can reuse."

Then another said, "we can reduce."

They all agreed to spend a day making Mother Earth happy before her birthday and then celebrate Earth Day

Day 10

Sunny the sun, found ways to conserve water. She says, "The less water each person uses, the less wastewater goes down to the ocean. If we stop dumping dirty water into places where clean water areas are, people can drink clean water.

Only open the water tap when needed, like to have a wash, drink water or clean our hands. Try storing some rain water in buckets or a rain barrel, which reduces run-off and can be used to water the plants in the yard, clean cars, and play with water puddles outside."

Day 9

Moony says, "I know what to do. Start putting all items bought at the market store into reusable shopping bags instead of plastics bags, and also help others around me reduce the use of plastics."

Day 8:

Mercuro says, "Start choosing healthy cleaning soaps and non-toxic chemicals in the house to keep the house clean and Mother Earth will be healthy and happy."

Day 7:

Veranus says, "I've got a great idea to make Mother earth happy on her day. Children can bike ride with their friends to school instead of going in their car. This helps reduce carbon dioxide coming out from car pipes."

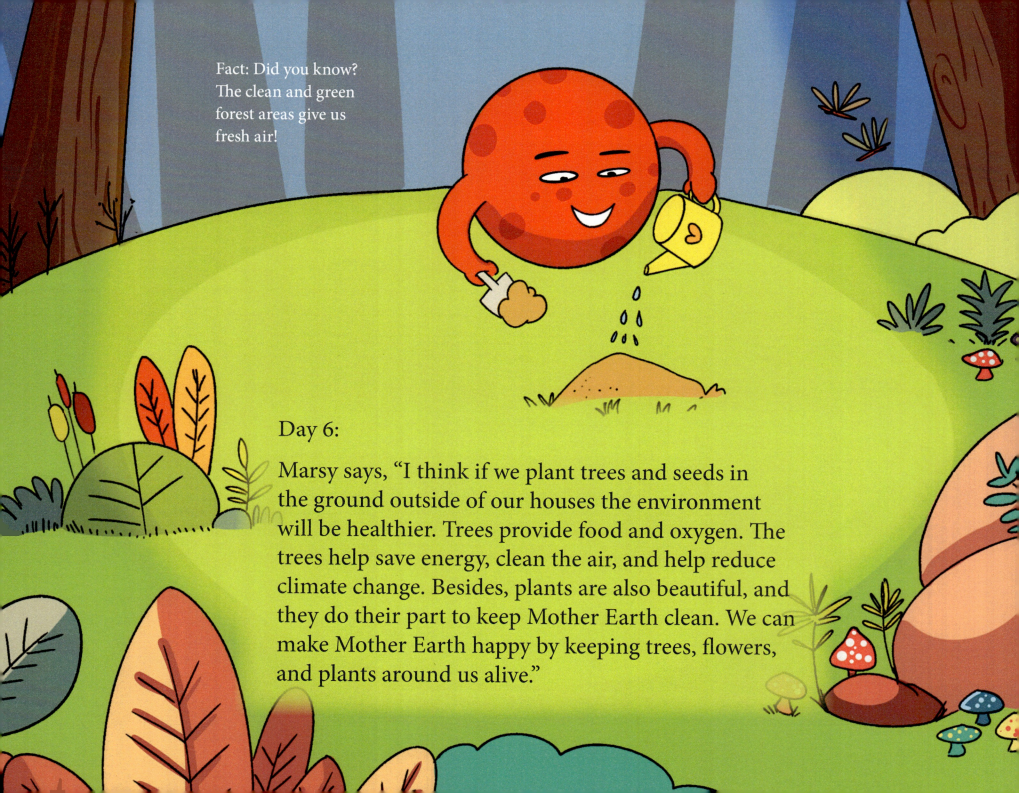

Fact: Did you know? The clean and green forest areas give us fresh air!

Day 6:

Marsy says, "I think if we plant trees and seeds in the ground outside of our houses the environment will be healthier. Trees provide food and oxygen. The trees help save energy, clean the air, and help reduce climate change. Besides, plants are also beautiful, and they do their part to keep Mother Earth clean. We can make Mother Earth happy by keeping trees, flowers, and plants around us alive."

Day 5

Jupitu the great, says, "We can increase efforts to reuse things around us, like straws, to-go cups, and reusable grocery bags. Each one we reuse over and over again reduces the stress on Mother Earth.

Fact: Can you believe that 20% of landfill waste is food? Do you know that composting reduces the volume in our landfills? Also, food waste buried in a landfill doesn't get enough oxygen and will produce strong gas. This is not healthy!

Day 4

Saturny says, "Compost food waste. If we collect all the left-over food and scraps and transfer them to the compost facility they can be safely converted to healthy dirt.

Day 3

Stary the superstar, says, "Keep plants, flowers and trees well nourished, growing healthy and strong by using the compost exposed to oxygen.

Instead of putting food in the garbage we need to keep some for the plants, we can use it for the plants in our gardens and Mother Earth will be happy and healthy, too."

Day 2

Uranusy says, "Hmm, go camping with friends and families and enjoy the quiet forests. When we spend time having fun, playing, and learning more about Earth then we can become happier, healthier, smarter, more creative, and better problem solvers. I know Mother Earth will love that so much. And, it will make the party so beautiful and clean on her birthday."

Day 1

Neptunes says "Actually we can reduce by cutting down on all waste at home, park, school and everywhere around us. Just like, for you to finish your food and to ask for what you can finish.

"You can just follow the three "R's" easily, just like my brothers and sisters have shown."

After the whole 10 days were completed everyone came together to celebrate Mother Earth.

Mother Earth saw all that her siblings and people were doing and felt so happy. She gave them a big hug and said this is the best Birthday Ever!

The End!

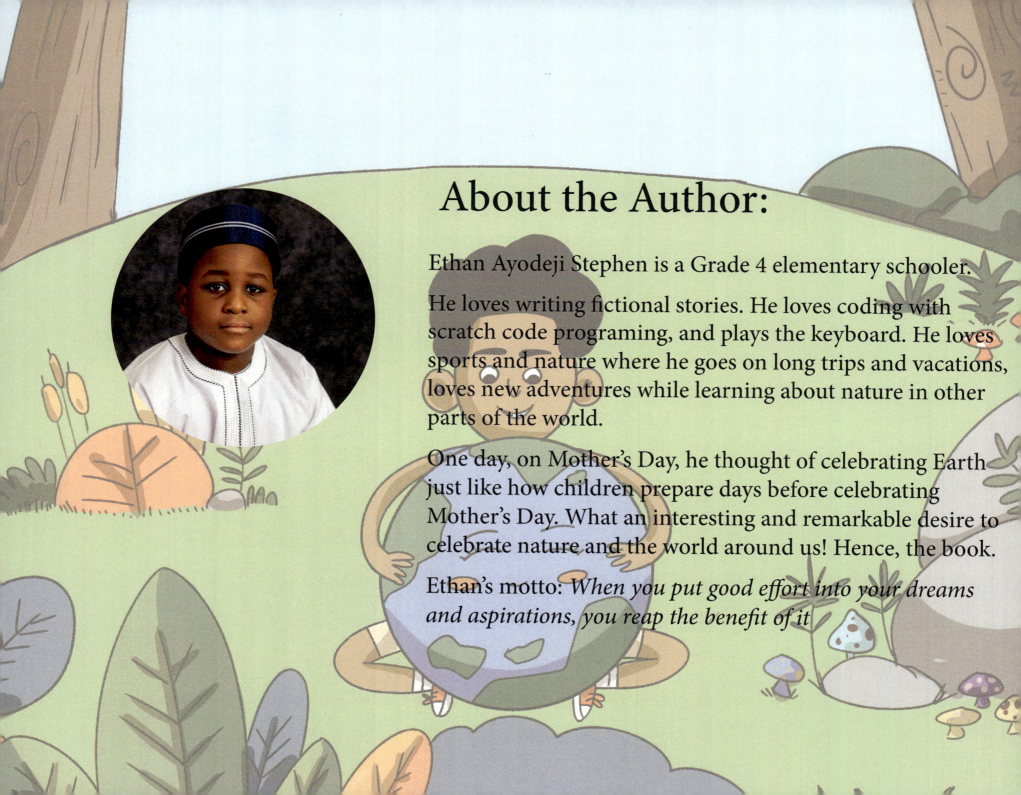

About the Author:

Ethan Ayodeji Stephen is a Grade 4 elementary schooler.

He loves writing fictional stories. He loves coding with scratch code programing, and plays the keyboard. He loves sports and nature where he goes on long trips and vacations, loves new adventures while learning about nature in other parts of the world.

One day, on Mother's Day, he thought of celebrating Earth just like how children prepare days before celebrating Mother's Day. What an interesting and remarkable desire to celebrate nature and the world around us! Hence, the book.

Ethan's motto: *When you put good effort into your dreams and aspirations, you reap the benefit of it*